Jack & the Beanstalk

A Folk Tale

Adapted by:
Ken Forsse
Margaret Ann Hughes

Illustrated by:
Russell Hicks
Douglas McCarthy
Theresa Mazurek
Allyn Conley-Gorniak
Julie Ann Armstrong

This Book Belongs To:

Use this symbol to match book and cassette.

Once upon a time there lived a boy named Jack. This was not Jack Be Nimble, or Jack Sprat, or Little Jack Horner. He was just plain "Jack."

Now Jack lived with his mother in a very small house. The clothes they wore were old and tattered...and they hardly ever had enough to eat. You see, Jack and his mother were very poor.

What little food they had left was almost gone. Jack's mother decided there was nothing left to do but sell their cow, Nellie.

So that morning Jack led Nellie down the dusty road to town. On his way, Jack met a peddler.

The peddler offered to buy Nellie the cow for five magic beans!

So Jack returned home with the beans, certain he had made a very good trade. But when Jack told his mother what he had done, she became very upset.

Jack's mother threw the beans out the window and sent Jack to his room.

Jack lay in his bed. He really wanted the beans to be magic. Jack was always telling his mother stories about magic things. Oh, if only those beans could have been magic.

The next morning, Jack awoke to a most unusual sight. A giant green leaf was poking through his open window. Jack threw on his clothes and ran outside. And there, growing out of the ground right where his mother had thrown the beans, was an enormous plant…it was a giant beanstalk!

Jack got his mother and showed her what had happened to the beans.

As Jack and his mother looked up, they couldn't even see the top of the beanstalk. It had grown right up through the clouds!

Jack was so excited that he started to climb up the stalk.

Jack climbed and climbed, higher and higher. He could see all over the countryside.

Higher and higher he climbed, until…Jack climbed right up through the clouds! The top of the clouds was like another land!

As Jack got off the beanstalk

and started to look around, he noticed a road that led off into the distance.

Jack started to follow the road. It led him over a hill and into a valley. In the valley there was a castle, the largest castle that Jack had ever seen. Jack walked right up to the castle and its enormous wooden door.

Jack knocked on the door.

From inside the castle came a tiny voice inviting Jack to enter.

Jack was barely able to reach the door handle. He unlatched the handle and pushed the door open.

Inside there was a very large room…with very large furniture. Jack looked around the room, but there was no one there.

Jack heard the tiny voice again. It was coming from a little orange hen. The hen was locked up in a cage that sat on a large chest.

The hen wanted Jack to let her out of the cage. Jack could not believe that the hen was actually talking.

The hen explained that she had been captured by the giant who owned the castle. Suddenly, Jack heard loud footsteps from outside.

The little hen had no trouble convincing Jack that he should not let the giant find him in the castle. Jack hid behind the large chest, just as the giant opened the door.

Oh, my! The giant was monstrous. He was at least twice as big as any man Jack had ever seen before. Jack was very frightened as he hid behind the chest. The giant picked up the cage that held the hen and put it on his table.

The giant told the hen that if she didn't lay golden eggs for him, he would cook her for his dinner. The poor little hen knew that the giant meant what he said, and she did her best to lay an egg.

Jack could not believe his eyes! The hen had laid a real golden egg!

The giant opened the cage and shook and shook the hen until she laid one golden egg after another. After the sixth egg, the poor little hen was just too tired to lay any more.

The giant shut the cage and put it back on the chest. Then he put the golden eggs into a large bag. The bag was almost overflowing…it had so many golden eggs in it.

Then the giant sat down in his chair and started to doze off.

Jack cautiously came out from behind the chest.

Because Jack had seen how mean the giant was, he knew he had to rescue the little hen. He opened the cage and took the hen out. Then, being very careful not to awaken the giant, Jack pulled open the heavy castle door.

With the hen under one arm, Jack ran as fast as he could down the road, away from the castle. All he could think about was saving the hen from the giant.

Just as Jack reached the beanstalk, he heard the footsteps of the giant.

Jack jumped onto the beanstalk and started climbing down it, still cradling the hen under his arm. Halfway down the stalk, Jack called to his mother to get the ax and start chopping down the beanstalk.

As Jack got to the ground, he grabbed another ax and helped his mother chop. Looking up, they saw the giant climbing down the beanstalk!

Finally the beanstalk started to lean to one side.

The giant quickly climbed back up the stalk and crawled back into the clouds, just as the beanstalk toppled over and fell to the ground.

First, an enormous beanstalk, then a giant, and finally a chicken that could talk…Jack's mother was beginning to believe in magic herself!

The little orange hen was so grateful to Jack for setting her free that she asked if she could stay with Jack and his mother forever.

Then she laid the biggest golden egg she had ever laid and gave it to them as a gift.

Jack, his mother and the little orange hen were very happy. With the golden egg they had plenty of money to buy food and clothes, and they shared their wealth with all who were less fortunate than they were.

And they even had enough money left over to buy back old Nellie the cow.

And they all lived happily ever after.